Chocolate-
Covered
Ants

Other Apple Paperbacks that you might enjoy:

Scared Silly
by Eth Clifford

I Spent My Summer Vacation Kidnapped into Space
by Martyn N. Godfrey

No Coins, Please
by Gordon Korman

The Mall from Outer Space
by Todd Strasser

Oh, Brother!
by Johnniece Marshall Wilson

Chocolate-Covered Ants

Stephen Manes

AN
APPLE
PAPERBACK

SCHOLASTIC INC.
New York Toronto London Auckland Sydney

ISBN 0-590-40961-1

Copyright © 1990 by Stephen Manes.
All rights reserved. Published by Scholastic Inc.
APPLE PAPERBACKS is a registered trademark of Scholastic Inc.

12 11 10 9 8 7 6 5   3 4 5 6/9

Printed in the U.S.A.   40 for Mary and the aunts

One

I admit it: The chocolate-covered ants were sort of my fault. They never would have happened if I hadn't said yes when my weird Aunt Fran called.

She was calling from the mall. She was actually calling my mom, but Mom wasn't home. So Fran told me about this birthday present she was thinking of buying my little brother Adam. She asked me if I thought Adam would like it. And dumb me, I said yes.

"Then I'm buying it and that's that," Fran said. "But remember, you are sworn to secrecy. This is supposed to be a surprise. If Adam isn't surprised when he gets this present, I am personally blaming you. Got that?"

"Sure." Keeping secrets from my little brother

1

didn't bother me. In fact, it was kind of fun. All I had to do to drive Adam crazy was remind him I knew what he was going to get for his birthday and he didn't.

"No, you don't," Adam declared.

"Yes, I do," I said.

"I bet you don't," Adam insisted.

"How much?" I said.

"How much what?" Adam asked.

"How much you want to bet?"

"A million dollars."

"Oh, yeah, right!" I snorted. "You really have a million dollars!"

Adam gave me this very serious look. "I'll bet you a nickel."

I laughed. "A nickel? I'm not going to tell you what you're getting for your birthday for a crummy nickel!"

"Because you don't know," Adam insisted.

"I certainly do," I repeated.

"Bet you don't," Adam said, and then the whole thing would start over again.

Sometimes he'd try to guess what the present was, but he never even came close. Besides, all I'd say was "maybe." Sometimes he'd try to trick me by saying "Prove it," but only somebody Adam's age would fall for that one. So I didn't have much trouble keeping Aunt Fran's secret.

On Adam's birthday, Fran came over in the afternoon with a big box covered with birthday paper. "Happy birthday!" she said as she handed it to Adam. She pointed to a card taped to the outside. "Read this first."

Adam frowned and looked at it. "When you play with this, remember your aunt. Love, Fran." Adam frowned harder. He didn't care much for mushy stuff.

"Isn't that nice?" Mom told him. "What do you say?"

"I don't even know what's in here yet," Adam protested.

"Adam!" Mom scolded.

"Thank you," Adam mumbled as he tore off the gift wrap. Mom shook her head and sighed.

Adam stared at the box. It had a cartoon ant on the front. The ant was holding something that looked like an aquarium. Only instead of fish, there were lots of ants running around inside. A balloon coming from the cartoon ant's mouth screamed LIVE ANTS! The sides of the box read ANT COLONY!

"Wow!" Adam shouted. "This is great! This is neat! This has to be the best birthday present ever in the entire world!"

My mom didn't exactly feel that way about it. From the looks of things, she thought it was pretty close to the worst. "Fran!" she moaned. "Fran! I cannot believe my sister would do a thing like this to me!"

"Oh, come on. It's cute," Aunt Fran said, flashing her big smile. "And appropriate. Remember that rock group, Adam and the Ants?

Their leader was Adam Ant. That's how I got the idea."

Mom shook her finger at my aunt. "Fran, if a single ant gets loose in the house, you are personally going to pay for an exterminator."

"I'm a single aunt," Fran said with a grin.

"Very funny," Mom grunted. When it comes to insects, Mom's attitude is basically swat 'em or spray 'em.

"Come on, Ellen, lighten up," Fran told her. "It's foolproof. The man at the store was positive. And it's educational. It says so right on the package. No exterminator required."

Mom just snorted. But my brother didn't pay her any attention. He was busy ripping the cellophane off the box. He didn't exactly do the neatest job in the world, but finally he got it open.

"Wow!" He couldn't believe his eyes. The ant colony inside was a clear plastic box on a red, white, and blue plastic stand. It looked sort of like a skinny aquarium. But instead of water, it was filled with a lot of sandy dirt. "Wow!" he repeated. "Neat!"

He pointed to a town of little plastic buildings on top of the dirt. "What's that supposed to be?" he asked me.

I looked. "Well, the building in the middle says 'Independants Hall.' "

My mother groaned.

"The big bell in front of it," I went on, "says

4

'Liberanty Bell.' That statue next to it — see the one with an ant holding a rifle?"

Adam looked closely. "Yeah."

"Well, that one says 'Ant Revere.' And the sign on that little mound says 'Bunker Anthill.' "

"I don't get it," Adam whined.

"Unfortunately, we do," my mom sighed. "Go ahead, Max. Explain it to Adam."

"Yeah," Adam whimpered. "Explain it to me."

Well, how was I going to do that? I mean, Adam's bright — *too* bright sometimes — but he's only in second grade. I tried anyway. "See, Adam, everything's supposed to be sort of the way it was in America before the Revolutionary War. Back when America was a colony of England. That's why this is an ant *colony*. Get it?"

"Sure," Adam said. He pretended to get it, but I knew he didn't. He also didn't get most of the stupid riddles in the little book that came in the box:

Who flew his kite in a lightning storm?
  Benjamin Franklant!
Who sewed the first ant colony flag?
  Bugsy Ross!
Why did Ant Revere ride so fast?
  He had ants in his pants!

But the stupid riddles weren't the stupidest thing about the ant colony. After Adam searched all through the box, he realized what was missing.

5

"I thought it said there were ants in here," he complained.

"There's a big aunt right over here," Fran joked.

Adam scowled. "But where are the ants in *here?*"

"Let's see," Fran said. She reached over and picked up the ant colony box. Then she pulled out a little card and handed it to Adam. "Here."

Adam stared at the card. He flipped it over. "I don't see any ants."

"Read the card, Adam," Aunt Fran told him.

"There are too many big words for me," Adam said. "You read it, Max."

I read out loud:

"You are now the proud owner of the American Legacy Ant Colony. This educational toy will give you thousands of hours of fun and enchantment. There's just one thing missing — your ants!

"Don't worry: Your ants are waiting for you, and they're absolutely free. To order them, simply fill out this card with your name and address. Then drop the card in any mailbox. No stamp is required. Your ants will arrive in four to six weeks."

"Four to six weeks!" Adam whined. "That's almost forever! I'm gonna go dig up some ants from the front yard."

"Oh, no you're not," Mom told him. "I'm not about to have any more holes in our lawn, thank you. What the Halvorsons' dog does out there is bad enough."

"All I'm going to do," Adam said firmly, "is dig up some ants."

"Wrong." Mom folded her arms across her chest and gave him her patented "Just try it, buster" look.

"It won't work, anyhow," I pointed out.

"Why not?" Adam demanded.

"It says right here on the back of the box: 'Use only certified American Legacy Ants in your Ant Colony. Other kinds of ants may damage the Colony and void your warranty.'"

"What does 'voider warranty' mean?" Adam demanded.

"It means the company won't fix it if it breaks. Or" — I kind of grinned at this one — "if ants get out somehow and we have to get an exterminator." Mom shot me a dirty look.

"I need ants, and I need them now!" Adam wailed.

"It's only about a month," Aunt Fran told him patiently. "You waited a whole year for your birthday. A month isn't anywhere nearly that long. And this way you'll have nice, clean, fresh ants, instead of ones that've been running around outside getting dirty in the yard."

"Okay, okay," Adam sighed. "Come on, Max. Fill this out, quick!"

"Sure." I took the pen from beside the phone. While I filled in the card, Adam grabbed his jacket from the closet.

"Let's go!" he cried.

"Let's go where?" I asked.

"Up the street! To the mailbox!"

"Right now?"

"Yeah! Right now! Come on!"

I gave Mom a look.

"Oh, why not?" she said. "May as well get this madness over with sooner than later."

"Have fun," said Aunt Fran.

"We will!" Adam shouted, and gave her a big kiss.

"See?" Fran told Mom. "It's a hit."

Mom scowled. "Not with me, it isn't. Adam, be sure to look both ways at the corner."

"Right, Mom!" he shouted as we walked out the door.

"Are these ants ever going to be great!" Adam kept insisting as we walked up the street. "I can't wait till they get here!"

"Then we can make chocolate-covered ants," I joked.

"Yuck!" he said. "There's no such thing."

"There is too," I replied. "My friend Larry has a can of them. Anyway, his parents do."

"He does not. Nobody eats chocolate-covered ants. That's stupid."

"Adam, I've *seen* them."

"I don't care. They've got to be fake. Nobody would eat chocolate-covered ants."

"Fine. Have it your way."

Never mind that I had seen the can at Larry's house. Never mind that Adam was just a little kid and didn't know about a lot of things. When Adam gets something in his head, there's no sense trying to argue with him.

We got to the mailbox. Adam made me lift him up so he could put the letter in all by himself. Little did I know at the time that his ants would come back to haunt me — along with the chocolate-covered ones.

Two

ANY other second-grader would more or less have forgotten all about those ants by the next morning. Any other second-grader would have moved on to his other birthday presents, like his new Little League bat or his major league underwear.

Not Adam. He had actually fixed up his room just for his ants. The first thing I noticed was a sign outside his bedroom door. His printing kind of ran downhill, but you could still read it. It said *Wellcome Ants!*

Inside, the ant colony had a place of honor at the front of his desk. On his big wall calendar, right below where it said *Birthday,* he had written *Sent For Ants!!!*

"When do you think those ants will show up?"

10

This was only the fiftieth time he'd asked me that question. "For the last time, Adam," I said, "it'll be four to six weeks."

But Adam wasn't going to believe a mere older brother. When we went into the kitchen for breakfast, he whined at Mom, "When do you think those ants will show up?"

Mom made a face. "I can tell you when I *wish* they'd show up."

"When?" Adam pleaded.

"The fourteenth of never."

Adam made a face. "Don't worry, Mom. They're going to be great. You never let us have pets before."

Mom frowned. "Ants are not pets. Ants are insects. If I find even a single ant on your lap or anybody else's, the whole colony is out of here."

"Don't worry. This is better than some old dog or cat. It's a whole colony. It's educational!" Adam reminded her.

"It'll be really educational if they get loose," I joked.

Mom looked horrified. "They'd better *not* get loose."

"They won't. The ant colony is double-sealed for your protection. The instructions say so."

Mom just sighed. "Sometimes I wish my sister wouldn't get so all-fired creative."

At school that day, Adam must have told every kid in his class about the ant colony. Probably half a dozen times. At least. After school, he brought three of his friends home with him to show the thing off. "Any mail for me?" he asked as he came through the kitchen door with them. "Any very important mail?"

"You've got to be kidding!" I told him. "Four to six weeks, remember? Twenty-eight days minimum!"

Adam made a face, passed out cookies and pop, and took his friends to his room. I kind of sneaked down the hall to listen in. By the time I got there, Adam was proudly showing off the ant colony.

"Neat, huh?" he bragged.

"It's neat, all right," said his best friend Harry, pressing his nose to the plastic. But Harry was the smartest kid in Adam's class, and it didn't take him long to figure out what was wrong. "But where are the ants?"

"They're coming," Adam said. "I ordered them from the factory. They'll be here any day now."

"You didn't tell us that!" said Harry. "You told us about all these ants running around in this colony!"

"Well, that's what there will be, soon," Adam replied.

"So we came over here to see invisible ants! Great!" his friend Thom said sarcastically. If it doesn't have something to do with sports, Thom isn't interested.

"*Imaginary* ants," Harry corrected him.

"*No* ants is more like it," said Ben sadly. Ben

was on his way to becoming a major nerd.

"All right, all right," Adam told them. "You just wait. See if I ever show you all the neat stuff my ants can do."

"That's okay," said Thom. "I've got an invisible dog, and I won't let you see him, either." Everybody laughed but Adam.

Don't ask me why, but every once in a while I kind of feel I have to stick up for my little brother. I poked my head in the door. "Hey, you guys, he's not kidding," I told his friends. "I sent the order in for the ants just yesterday. He's going to get a whole mess of them. He's even going to get some special attack ants. If you don't watch out, he'll train them to swarm all over you."

"Attack ants!" sneered Harry. "There's no such thing."

"You wait," I said. "You'll see."

"I think Adam has ants in his pants," Thom teased.

"Yeah. Ants in his pants," Ben echoed. "Right."

Everybody giggled but Adam and me. "Just you wait," Adam told his friends. "Sooner or later you'll be sorry you ever made fun of my ant colony."

"Yeah, guys," I said. "You'll see. You'd better watch out for those attack ants. If I were you, I'd practice up on self-defense."

Adam took me aside after they had left. "Max, am I really going to get attack ants?"

13

"No," I told him. "I just made that up."

Adam looked kind of disappointed.

"Hey, don't look so glum about it," I said. "You won't get any chocolate-covered ants, either."

But for a long time he didn't get any ants at all. Every morning for weeks and weeks Adam would come into the kitchen for breakfast and say, "Boy, I sure hope those ants come today."

I would always answer, "Me too, because then you'd stop bothering me about them." We should have videotaped the conversation and saved ourselves some breath.

But Adam's ant-craziness wasn't all bad as far as I was concerned. Usually it was my job to take in the mail and the UPS packages; now I didn't have to bother. Every afternoon Adam would dash home after school, run to the mailbox, and flip through every piece of mail. He'd even look at the postcards, just to make sure they didn't have some kind of news about his ants. Then he'd run around the side of the house where the UPS man hides packages in the bushes. Finally he'd come inside, all disappointed that his ants hadn't arrived.

But that didn't stop Adam. You know how little kids get ideas in their heads? It's almost as if some mysterious force comes over them. One day they're halfway normal. The next day all they can talk about is dinosaurs. Or the Titanic. Or the Eiffel Tower. Or monsters. Well, this time with my little brother it was ants.

He went to the school library and took out every single book they had on ants. Then he read all the ant articles in the encyclopedia. He didn't understand most of the words — hey, *I* didn't understand a lot of them — but he started to collect all these weird ant facts. And every chance he got, he would tell them to anybody stupid enough to listen.

We'd go outside to play catch, and Adam would say, "You know what, Max?"

"What?"

"The ant's body is divided into three main parts."

"Throw me a grounder," I'd shout.

"They are: the head, the thorax, and the abdomen."

"Fascinating, Adam," I'd holler. "Throw the ball."

"Okay. But don't step on any ants!"

Naturally, I'd pretend to stomp every anthill in the yard. It would really drive him crazy.

But he drove *me* crazy without even trying. We'd be watching some show on TV, and out of the blue Adam would say, "You know what, Max?"

"If it's about ants, I don't want to know it."

"Did you know the queen ant is the biggest one in the nest? She is the only one who lays the eggs that hatch into baby ants."

"Thank you, Adam. Now would you please shut up so I can watch this show?"

"Do you want to know something about worker ants?"

"No," I'd say. But Adam would tell me anyway.

Even at the dinner table — *especially* at the dinner table — Adam would come up with some not-so-amazing-once-you'd-heard-it-seventeen-times-already fact. For example: "Did you know there are at least one quadrillion ants living on the face of the earth? That's one with fifteen zeroes after it. That's one, zero, zero, zero — "

"Adam, we get the picture," Mom said.

" — zero, zero, zero, ze — "

"Come on, Adam. Eat your dinner and shut up," I said.

" — ro, zero, zero, zero, zer — "

Mom shook her head. "Adam, you have told us this at least one quadrillion times already."

" — o, zero, zero, zero — " he paused for breath and gave us a big grin " — zero."

"Zero is how much dessert you are going to have if you don't eat the rest of your chicken," Mom said. "Which reminds me: Please don't tell me about those ants that regurgitate their food. Thank you."

Three

I was just sitting down in the kitchen for an after-school snack when I heard an ear-piercing shriek from outside. I went into the living room and looked out the window. The shrieking was coming from Adam. He was holding a little cardboard box and jumping up and down. "My ants are here!" he kept shouting. "My ants are here! Wow!"

I went back into the kitchen. Adam came in waving the box around. "Hey, Max! Look! My ants are here!"

"I heard," I said. "Half the neighborhood probably heard."

"You want to watch me put them into the ant colony?"

"You remember what Mom said: You're not allowed to do that by yourself."

"Oh, yeah," he grumbled. "Then come and help me."

"Why should I?" If there is one thing fun about having a little brother, it's being able to torment him once in a while.

"Come on, Max."

"Maybe when I finish my snack," I said. "Maybe."

"I'll do it myself if you don't."

"I'll tell Mom if you do," I said. "You know how happy she is about this whole ant thing."

"Then finish eating and help me," he begged.

I didn't say anything. I just took nice long bites out of my cookie and chewed just slow enough to drive Adam nuts. "Come on, Max, finish eating. Please?"

"Em eetng fstas I cn," I said, which was annoy-your-brother-mouth-full talk for "I'm eating as fast as I can."

Adam stared at his package. One end was slightly bashed in. "This box looks kind of crinkled," he said. "You think these ants are okay?"

"How should I know?" I answered. "Maybe they're dead."

Adam looked horrified. "They're not! They can't be!"

"Sure they can," I said. "They could have frozen to death. They could have been run over by a truck. They could have been squashed somehow."

"The box doesn't look all that squashed," Adam

decided. "They've got to be okay. So come on, Max. Hurry up!"

"One last bite." I definitely made it last.

"See what happens next time you need help," he whined.

"Adam, you've waited this long. Another couple of minutes aren't going to matter. Let me see the box."

He handed it over. "Be careful."

"Sure," I said. "Now go get the ant colony from your room and take it into the bathroom."

"The bathroom?"

"Remember? Mom said we were supposed to handle the ants in the bathtub? That way if they get out or something, we can wash 'em down the drain?"

Adam went wild. "We are not washing my ants down any drain!"

"Only in case of emergency."

"I am not washing any ants down that drain!" Adam screamed.

"Calm down. Take it easy. If everything goes right, you won't have to. Now come on. No more fooling around. Go get the colony."

As Adam trudged off, I noticed that the box of ants was sealed with heavy tape. I ducked into my room to get my Swiss army knife. By the time I got to the bathroom, Adam was already there.

"Okay," I said. "Put the ant colony in the tub — over there, near the drain."

"Remember what I told you about washing ants down the drain," he warned.

"Don't worry," I said. "Now get ready. I'm going to open the package." I stabbed the tape with my knife.

"Watch out!" Adam shrieked.

"What's wrong now?"

"You might cut some of the ants!"

"We've got plenty of little Band-Aids," I joked.

"Max!"

"Just kidding."

"You'd better be," Adam said.

I sliced the tape and opened the flaps on the box. Inside was a smaller box, sealed with more plastic tape. It had the words **WARNING! READ ALL INSTRUCTIONS BEFORE OPENING** in red all over it.

"Where are the instructions?" asked Adam.

"Right here," I said. "On this little paper."

"What does it say?"

"It says 'Instructions.' "

Adam scowled. "Come on, Max."

"Okay. Here's what it says. It says, 'Your official American Legacy Ants are supplied in the enclosed hermetically sealed package. Here is how to get your ants into their new home.' "

"Well?" Adam demanded.

I started to read the instructions, but not out loud.

"Well?" he pressed.

"You know where the Food Flaps are on your ant colony?" I asked.

"Sure!" he said, and flipped a little door open. "There's one on the inside, too. That's double protection. So the ants don't get out when you feed them."

"Okay. Flip the other one open, too." He did. "Good. Now go out to the kitchen and get a piece of bread or a couple of lumps of sugar or something. You're supposed to put food in there to attract the ants."

"*You* go get it. I'll watch the ants."

I gave Adam one of my patented "If you don't do what I tell you, there's going to be trouble" looks, so he went. While he headed for the kitchen, I read the rest of the instructions. I figured if there was anything else we'd need from the kitchen, I ought to find out now so I could yell and make Adam bring it. I knew better than to try and stick him with two trips. But food was all we needed.

Adam came back with a piece of bread, a lump of sugar, and a huge pickle. "I thought ants liked sweet stuff," I said. "You think the pickle's a good idea?"

"The bread and sugar are for the ants. The pickle's for me." And he stuck it into his mouth.

"I thought you were in a hurry."

"Yeah, but I'm hungry, too," he said with his mouth full.

"Come on. Roll the bread into little tiny dough-balls," I told him.

"Sort of ant-sized, right?" he said, rolling bread between his fingers.

"Right. So it'll fit through the holes in the Food Flaps. I'll cut up the sugar so it'll fit, too." And that's what I did.

"These bread balls are kind of yucky," Adam said. "They turned funny colors from the dirt on my fingers."

"Now you know why Mom keeps telling you to wash your hands."

Adam made a face.

"Go ahead. Put 'em in," I said. "I don't think ants mind eating yuck."

"They eat worse stuff than this," Adam informed me. "Some ants chew up leaves. They spit them out and use what they spit out to grow fungus on. And then they eat the fungus."

I made a face. "Did you just make that up?"

"Honest! I read it in a library book," Adam said very seriously. "Except I don't think these ants are that kind of ant. I don't know, though. Maybe I'll put some leaves in the colony just to see what happens."

"Let's get them in there first. You ready?"

Adam nodded.

"Okay, listen up. Once I open the plastic on this box of ants, a little spout kind of thing is supposed to stick out. I need to put it in the Food Flap holes and push the ants out of the box. You watch and make sure the ants start coming out. Okay?"

"Yes," Adam said.

I ripped the tape from one end of the box and pulled out the little spout. I stuck it into the Food Flap holes. Then I pushed the end of the box to get the ants moving.

"Ants!" Adam cried.

There were ants, all right. Ants aplenty. Ants galore. They swarmed out of the spout and headed every which way in the colony. They crawled over the bread balls and the sugar hunks.

"These are some hungry ants," I said.

"They probably ate up all their food on the trip," Adam said. Then he shouted, "Wow! There's the queen!" He pointed to an ant that was bigger than all the rest. "It's just like in the books! This is great!"

I held the box tight against the ant colony so that none of the ants could turn around and get out. The ants just kept coming. They crawled up and down Independants Hall and the Liberanty Bell and the statue of Ant Revere. They dug in the sandy dirt. And finally they stopped swarming from the box.

"Maybe we should close the Food Flaps," Adam said.

"Wait a second. I want to make sure no more ants decide to sneak out."

"But what if some of the other ones decide to go back into the box? Maybe they think it's their home."

"I don't know . . ."

"Look! That guy's thinking about it."

One ant did look as though he might make a break for it. "Okay," I said. "Get ready to close the flaps."

"I'm ready."

"Now!" I said, and yanked the box from the hole. Adam clicked the inside flap shut, and then the one on the outside. I set the box in the tub and double-checked the Food Flaps to make sure Adam had closed them tight.

"Look!" Adam cried. "Another one!"

The ant box wasn't empty after all. A tiny little ant was climbing up the spout and looking around. "We've got to get him into the colony!" Adam said.

"Then pick him up before he gets loose," I said. "Either he goes into the colony, or we'll have to squoosh him."

"No!" Adam screamed. "We're not squooshing any of my ants!"

"Pick him up, then," I said. "Come on!"

Adam grabbed the ant from behind and held it while it squirmed around. I opened the Food Flaps. "Hurry up before they start crawling out! Put him on your finger and shove him in!"

The ant kept crawling up toward Adam's arm rather than down toward the flaps. But somehow Adam managed to drop the ant through the hole and onto the Liberanty Bell. I closed both Food Flaps and relaxed.

"Hey! Look!" Adam pointed. "Did you see that?"

I saw it, all right. An ant was in the tub, crawling toward the drain. Adam reached in and tried to grab it. Too late.

Adam went crazy. "It's your fault!" he cried, feeling around in the drain. "You lost one of my ants!"

"I didn't lose him," I said. "Neither one of us saw him in time. And anyhow, he had to be a really stupid ant. He didn't know what was good for him."

"My ants aren't stupid. And it was your fault! You lost him!"

I scowled. "Adam, take the ant colony out of the tub."

"What are you going to do?"

"Never mind. Just pick up the colony."

"Why?"

"Come on! Do it!" I shouted.

Adam did.

I turned the hot water on full blast. "You're drowning my lost ant!" Adam cried.

"You're darned tootin' I am." I tore open the ant box and rinsed it into the tub the way the instructions said to. A couple more ants washed down the drain.

"You drowned even more!" Adam whined. "I'm gonna tell Mom."

"Go ahead," I said. "Mom's not happy about this ant thing to begin with. If she finds out even one ant got loose, she might just make you take the whole colony back to Aunt Fran."

I could tell Adam understood. But now he was mad at me. It didn't matter that I'd helped him get his ants into the colony. It didn't matter that the ants were swarming around inside and digging holes and everything was just fine. Adam was mad, and when Adam got mad, that was the end of that.

Adam picked up the ant colony, carried it into his room, and slammed the door. He didn't even thank me for helping him. And he left it to me to clean the tub and take the empty ant box out to the garbage. That wasn't exactly something I hadn't expected. Little brothers are really great at getting out of cleaning up messes they've made.

When I got back from the garbage bin, Adam poked his head into the hall and shouted, "My ants are doing all sorts of neat things!"

"Like what?" I shouted back.

"You won't find out! I'm not going to let you see them! You're an ant-killer!"

Actually, I didn't care all that much if he let me see his ants or not. But I was beginning to get kind of tired of his attitude. Adam stuck his tongue out at me and hollered "Ant-killer!" at the top of his lungs. Then he slammed the door again.

That kid was really getting on my nerves. I decided I'd have to teach him a lesson. And I thought of a really great way to do it.

Four

"MOM!" Adam screamed when he heard her come through the door. "Mom! The ants are here! The ants are here! Come look!" He ran to the living room and grabbed her by the arm.

"Do I have to?" Mom asked wearily.

"Yes! Come on!" Adam said, dragging her along.

"Okay, Adam, okay," Mom replied. "I can get there under my own power, thank you."

"Well, hurry up!"

I followed along right behind them. Since I was officially an ant-killer, Adam still hadn't let me see the colony.

"Look, Mom!" he squealed. "Aren't they great?"

Mom scowled. "Great is not exactly the word I'd use, no."

"See those two? I named them Harry and Thom." Only my little brother would come up with the idea of naming his ants.

"How can you tell them apart?" Mom asked.

"Harry has a bigger thorax. The thorax is the main part of an ant's body, not counting the wings and the head and stuff. See? Harry's is bigger than Thom's."

Mom shook her head. "They all look the same to me."

"They're not the same. Every one is different. See that one there — the one climbing on the statue?"

Mom nodded.

"That's Willoughby. And the one on the Liberanty Bell is Julius Caesar."

"Come on," I said. "You can't really tell which one's which!"

"Can too," Adam said.

"What's that one's name?" I said, pointing.

"Which one?"

"The one right there — beside the statue of John Hantcock."

"That one doesn't have a name yet."

"Can I name him?" Mom said. "Or is it a her?"

"It's a him, Mom. Don't you know anything? There's only one queen for the whole colony."

"I knew that," Mom said, "but I forgot. Can I name him or can't I?"

Adam thought it over. "I don't know . . . "

"I've got a really good name."

"What is it?" Adam asked.

"Little Anthony."

Adam made a face. "Little Anthony? Little Anthony? What's so good about that name?"

"It has 'ant' in it," Mom said.

"So?"

"Well, it's also the name of this singer from back in the fifties . . . never mind. It's too hard to explain."

"I think you should name them all Ted," I said. "That way you wouldn't have to worry about telling them apart."

"Very funny, you ant-killer," Adam snarled.

"Adam!" Mom exclaimed. "What kind of talk is that?"

"Max killed some of my ants!"

"He did?"

"He certainly did."

"Is that true, Max?"

I sighed. "Thanks, Adam. Thanks a lot."

"You killed my ants. You know you did."

Mom stared at me. "Well?"

I shook my head. "What really happened is that when we were filling up the ant colony in the bathtub, a couple of ants got away."

"*How* many?" Mom demanded.

"Really — only one or two. They crawled down the drain and we couldn't reach them. So I had to flush them down with hot water. It's what the instructions said to do."

"Is that true, Adam?"

"Yeah. He killed them!"

Mom gave Adam a hard stare. "As far as I'm concerned, Adam, Max did exactly the right thing." I stuck my tongue out at him behind Mom's back as she went on. "And you remember, Adam: If even one ant gets out of there, the colony disappears for good. I don't care what they're called. None of those ants is allowed out of the colony. Ever. Period. You got it?"

Adam nodded.

"Good," Mom said. "Now, this is fast-food night. You two figure out where you want to go for dinner."

"Somewhere where they serve chocolate-covered ants," I said.

Mom groaned. "Five minutes. Be ready." And she walked out the door.

"You better not try anything with my ants, Max," Adam warned.

"Bet they'd be delicious under hot-fudge sauce," I teased. "Or like candy. Chocolate-covered ants. Yum." I smacked my lips.

"You'd better not, Max. I'm warning you."

"I guess I'll just have to buy a can of them, then. I've suddenly got this horrible craving for chocolate-covered ants!"

"Max, you're making that up. Nobody eats chocolate-covered ants. Nobody!"

"Anteaters might."

"Maybe. But people don't."

I chuckled. "Well, smarty-ants, I guess you don't know everything about ants, then."

"I do, too. Almost, anyway. And I've never heard of chocolate-covered ants. Ever. You're making this up, Max."

I shook my head. "They're a special kind of ant that's dipped in chocolate. They're supposed to be very unusual and delicious."

"You're making this up," Adam snarled. "I know you are."

"How much?" I said calmly.

"How much what?"

"How much you want to bet?"

"PEOPLE DON'T EAT ANTS!" Adam screamed. "THEY DON'T!"

"You're wrong, Adam. I told you before. I've seen them. Anyway, I've seen the can."

"Where?"

"At Larry's."

"You're lying," Adam said. "I just know you're lying."

"Why would I want to lie about a thing like this?"

"I don't know, but you are."

"Adam, stop calling me a liar. If you're so sure I'm wrong, let's bet on it! Come on. How much?"

"People don't eat ants. Not even chocolate-covered ones. I'd bet my whole ant colony on it."

"I don't want your dumb ant colony. How much money do you have saved up?"

Adam thought it over. "Thirteen dollars and a bunch of pennies."

"Forget your pennies. We'll make it thirteen dollars even."

Adam looked thoughtful. "Yeah, but what if I lose?"

"You just said you were sure you wouldn't lose. You said you were sure people didn't eat chocolate-covered ants. And if you're right, you'll get thirteen dollars." Which was actually a little more than I had at the moment. I am not too good when it comes to saving money.

"Yeah, but what if I lose?"

"Then I get your thirteen dollars."

"But that's all the money I have."

"You'd still have all your pennies."

Adam thought it over. He kept looking at his ant colony and then back at me. He couldn't make up his mind.

I was just hoping he wouldn't chicken out. I was getting sick and tired of Adam and his ants and being called an ant-killer in front of Mom. This bet would definitely teach him a lesson. And I could make a little money besides. I mean, I had *seen* that can of ants with my own eyes. There was no way I was going to lose.

"Okay," Adam said. "But you can't just *tell* me

32

people eat these things. I want to *see* people eating them."

"Fine," I told him. "No problem." If I had to, I'd eat them myself. My philosophy about food is that I'll try anything once.

"And you have to do it soon. I'm tired of waiting around for ant stuff."

"Sure," I said cockily. "You'll have your proof by the end of the week. Friday at the latest." It was Monday now; there was no reason I couldn't round up Larry's ants and munch a couple of 'em in the next day or two. "But one more thing. Neither one of us can mention our bet to Mom. If you tell her about it, you lose the bet. If I tell her about the bet, then I lose it."

"Why?"

"It's none of her business, that's why. It's just between you and me. Now is it a deal or isn't it?"

I extended my hand. Adam looked at it suspiciously.

"Come on, Adam. Shake on it. Or don't."

"Okay," Adam said, grabbing my hand. "But remember, you have to show me that people eat chocolate-covered ants. I don't just want you to bring over a book that says they do."

"Adam, you have just kissed thirteen dollars good-bye," I told him.

"We'll see," my little brother replied. Then he turned back to his ants.

Mom stuck her head in the door. "Where are we going to eat?"

33

"Ant King," I suggested.

My brother screamed, so we didn't. Besides, Adam reminded us all the way there that there *is* no ant king — only a queen. So we ended up at Dairy Queen.

As I wolfed down my burger, I made my plans for winning the bet and making Adam shut up. What I had to do was go over to my friend Larry's house. I had to borrow the can of chocolate-covered ants, bring them home, and eat a couple in front of Adam. Then he could smash his piggy bank and pay me. It'd be easy — except for actually eating those ants.

So the minute we got back home, I phoned Larry. "Hey, Lar, what's shakin'?"

"Jell-O. What's shakin' around your place?"

"My little brother's going to shake plenty if you can help me out."

"Okay, if you help *me* out. I'm stuck on a couple of these weird fractions in our homework for Milken."

"It's a deal. But first things first. Remember that can of chocolate-covered ants you had at your place?"

"I sure do. Matter of fact, I saw it a couple of weeks ago."

I smiled. Adam was in big trouble now. "No kidding!"

"Yeah. You'll never guess what my parents did with it."

I suddenly had this funny feeling in the pit of

my stomach. "Did they eat the ants?" I squeaked.

"Eat them? Are you kidding?"

I breathed a sigh of relief. "So what *did* they do with them?"

"They sent them to their aunt. You know, for kind of a gag gift. Ants? Aunt? Get it?"

"I get it, all right." All of a sudden I didn't feel so hot. "Can you get 'em back?"

"I doubt it. My aunt lives in Greece. You remember when you met her last summer? That trip was the first time she'd been back to the United States in about ten years."

"Great," I said, meaning anything but that.

"So what is it you wanted me to help you out with?"

I told him the whole story so he'd understand why I needed chocolate-covered ants in kind of a hurry.

"You're crazy. Adam will never pay even if you do win."

"We'll see. Maybe your parents would know where I could get some of those ants?"

"I'll ask," Larry said. "But don't hold your breath. I think somebody gave 'em to *them* as a gag. Somehow I don't think people ever buy chocolate-covered ants for themselves. Not when there are potato chips and corn chips and cheese puffs in this world."

"Ask anyway," I said.

"Okay. Now what about those homework problems?"

"I'll have to go get my book." Then this awful idea suddenly popped into my head. "Wait a minute. I just thought of something. Maybe it was *all* a gag. Do you know if there were real ants in there?"

"In our homework?"

"In the can."

"You saw it for yourself. That's what it said: Chocolate-Covered Ants."

"Yeah, I know. But were they real ants or fake ants?"

"It's not like I checked out the ingredients, Max. The label didn't say chocolate-covered fake ants, did it?"

"But if the whole thing was just for gags, maybe they were just chocolate-covered caramels *shaped* like ants. You know, like those gummy worms and bugs."

"Well, I can't exactly open the can to find out," Larry said.

"Ask your parents, okay?"

"Okay, I'll ask. I'll tell you about it in home-room tomorrow. Now what about those fractions?"

I went and got my math book, thinking this ant business wasn't going to be quite as easy as I'd planned. Big deal. I still wasn't worried. I wasn't going to panic. I had plenty of antics up my sleeve. Even if I didn't have a fraction of an idea what they were.

Five

"I'VE got good news and bad news," Larry told me in homeroom next morning.

"About the ants?" I asked excitedly.

Larry nodded. "You want the good news or the bad news?"

I thought it over. "The good news."

"Okay. The good news is my mom thinks they're probably real ants. She said she's enough of a chocolate nut that if she had thought the things were only *shaped* like ants, she'd've eaten them for sure."

"Any more good news?"

"Well, my mom said you should probably be able to buy the ants someplace."

"I guess that's sort of good news," I said. "Any more?"

"Only the bad news. My mom and dad have no idea where you can buy them. They got that can as a gift at a party sometime. It was so long ago, they don't even remember who gave it to them."

I frowned. "Bad news, all right."

"Like I said," Larry reminded me, "nobody buys chocolate-covered ants for themselves."

But I had to find a way to buy chocolate-covered ants for myself — or my little brother would teach *me* a lesson. And I had to do it by Friday.

The minute I got home, I went into Mom's bedroom and locked the door. We're not supposed to lock the doors to the bedrooms, so we won't get trapped inside — it happened one time when I was a real little kid, and they had to call the fire department to get me out — but just this once I wanted absolute privacy. I was not going to let Adam walk in and find out what I was doing.

I picked up the Yellow Pages and flipped through it to "Ants." There were listings for "Antennas," "Antifreeze Compounds," and "Antiques," but that was it. There were no listings for ants at all.

I thought about what Larry had said. If his parents got the ants as a gift, it made sense that maybe they came from a gift shop. So I looked under "Gift Shops."

There must have been a hundred listings. I

didn't have any idea where to start, so I started at the beginning. I dialed the first number on the page.

"Adams Gift Shop," said a friendly woman's voice.

"I'm looking for something kind of, uh, special," I said nervously.

"All our gifts are special," the woman said. "Can I ask who you're buying it for?"

"Well, it's sort of for my little brother," I said, suddenly feeling kind of embarrassed. "It's a surprise. I want to get him some, uh, chocolate-covered, uh, ants."

"Very funny" was the next thing I heard. And a loud bang as the woman hung up.

Mom always says you have to try, try again. So I phoned the next name on the list. "Always Gifts," said a deep male voice.

I decided to get right to the point this time. "Do you sell chocolate-covered ants?" I asked.

This time all I heard was the hangup. People obviously thought I was joking.

That's when I got a different idea. Since the ants were chocolate-covered, maybe the place to get them was a candy store. I flipped through the Yellow Pages to "Candy." There were plenty of listings.

This time I started from the bottom and worked up. It didn't help much. I made half a dozen calls, but nobody had ever even heard of chocolate-covered ants, or at least they wouldn't admit it. About half the people thought I was just some kid trying to be funny over the phone, and hung up. I tried one more time.

"Do you sell chocolate-covered ants?"

"Chocolate-covered *whats*?" The guy on the other end of the line sounded as though if you saw him he'd have a twinkle in his eye.

"Ants. Chocolate-covered ants."

"Oh. I thought you said chocolate-covered *pants*. We do have those from time to time, especially when we spill the stuff on ourselves. But we don't sell them."

"But what about ants?"

"I'm afraid we don't. We have gummy spiders and tarantulas. No ants, though. Sorry."

"Maybe you know where I could get chocolate-covered ants? It's important."

"Is this some sort of scavenger hunt?"

"No," I said. "It's more important than that."

"Well, if you put a chocolate bar out in your backyard, you'd have ant-covered chocolate soon enough, wouldn't you? But that's not what you asked for."

"It sure isn't," I agreed.

"Wait a minute!" the man said. "Do you mean those chocolate-covered ants that come in a little can?"

My heart skipped a beat. "Right. That's exactly what I'm talking about."

"I remember those. The can used to say 'Gourmet Delicacy.' Chocolate-covered ants. I wonder whatever happened to them."

"You don't sell them?"

"I haven't seen those things since I was a kid."

"Do you have any idea where I could get some?"

"Not the slightest. For all I know, they're no longer made. But maybe I'm wrong. Oh, here's a customer. Well, good-bye. Good luck with your hunt." He hung up.

It was hopeless. Chocolate-covered ants were a lot rarer than I thought. Maybe they didn't even exist anymore.

I raided my savings stash, which I kept in the back of my closet in an old tin can. I spilled the money on the bed. I counted it out. It came to six dollars and seventy-three cents. Even with next week's allowance, I wouldn't have enough to pay Adam if I lost.

I was less than worthless. Less than zero.

Or maybe not. . . .

Six

My Mom is big on homemade stuff. She says if you can't afford to buy a present, you can make one of your own. She even made a pretty good imitation of a fast-food hamburger at home once, back when I was Adam's age and I refused to eat anything else for some strange little-kid reason.

So maybe I couldn't buy chocolate-covered ants, but I sure could try to make my own. I figured the best way to start was to make that ant-covered chocolate the man from the candy store had mentioned.

I dug up a big old chocolate bar from the stash I kept in my room for special occasions. I put it in my pocket to warm it up a little and get it nice and gooshy. And then I went outside to find some ants.

If you had told me just last week that today I'd be out in the yard hunting for ants, I would have said you were crazy. Nuts. Cuckoo. Now here I was, the Great Ant Hunter. As I went out the front door, I was the one who felt crazy.

But at least I knew where the anthills were in our front yard. Adam had dragged me around to every one of them one day while he was waiting for his official ants to arrive. It didn't take me long to find a cone where ants were crawling in and out.

I unwrapped my chocolate bar, mushed it up a little, and stuck it down on the anthill. A couple of minutes later the chocolate bar started to look all fuzzy. From one end to the other, ants were marching up and down on it.

If I carried it into the house like that, some of the ants might drop off on the way to the kitchen. That could get me in real trouble with Mom. So I went back inside to get a plastic bag.

On my way out again, I ran into Adam at the front door. "What are you doing?" he asked.

"None of your business." I walked over to the anthill.

Adam followed me. "Oooh! Yuck! That candy bar is covered with ants!"

"Good thinking." I picked it up, put it in the plastic bag, and sealed the whole thing with a twist-tie.

"You're not going to bring that into the house, are you?"

"I sure am."

"You know what Mom says about ants. I'm gonna tell."

"Go ahead. But remember, if you tell her about our bet, you lose."

Adam followed me inside. "What are you gonna do with those ants?"

"What do you *think* I'm going to do? I'm going to turn them into chocolate-covered ants. Then I'm going to eat them. And then you're going to owe me thirteen dollars."

"Now I'm really gonna tell," Adam said.

"Who? There's nobody around *to* tell."

"I'm gonna phone Mom at work."

"You know you're only supposed to do that in an emergency."

"Well, this is an emergency. You're gonna get ants all over the place."

"No, I'm not," I said.

"Yes, you are. Look! They're crawling all around the bag."

That much was true. The ants *were* crawling all around the inside of the bag. I hadn't counted on that. I thought they would just stay on the chocolate bar so I could sort of mash them into it and kill them and then eat them. Now if I opened the bag, chances were pretty good that some of the ants would escape.

I put the bag in the kitchen sink to make sure

I could wash down any ants that happened to get out. Just to see what would happen, I tried mashing a couple of them through the bag by pressing my finger against it. They died with a tiny little crunch.

"Ant-killer!" Adam cried.

I actually felt pretty bad about it. I don't like being mean to animals. I just hoped if I started on ants it wouldn't lead to bigger things, like kicking cats or something. But somehow I didn't think so.

Still, it would take an awful lot of work to kill all these ants. And I realized I wouldn't have the stomach to eat them even if I could. I mean, these would be squooshed ants from my front yard. Who knew where they might have been lately — maybe our garbage cans, where they'd been eating the stuff we threw away a week ago. I didn't want to think about swallowing these poor guys.

And even if I squooshed ants till suppertime, some of them would probably still be alive. My philosophy is I'll eat anything once, but that doesn't include live stuff, except maybe oysters, and the one time I ate a live oyster was plenty.

Just to make matters worse, my little brother kept yelling "Ant-killer! Ant-killer!" at the top of his lungs. It gave me a great idea. A brilliant idea. I could melt the chocolate, roast the ants, and sort of sterilize them — or at least make them as sanitary as ants get — all at once. I set the microwave oven for three minutes and opened the door.

"You can't do that!" Adam shouted.

"No? Just watch me!"

I stuck the plastic bag in the microwave oven. Then I shut the door and pressed the start button. The buzz sounded and the light went on inside.

"I can't believe you are doing this!" my brother shouted. "All those ants are going to die!"

I couldn't believe I was doing this, either. It was cruelty to animals, sort of. But on the other hand, I was doing it to eat them. It wasn't any crueler than boiling a live lobster or crab or oyster, really. And ants were even lower forms of life. If it hadn't been for my little brother — and he was a pretty low form of life himself — I wouldn't be giving it a second thought.

Of course, if it weren't for my little brother, I wouldn't be doing this at all. I mean, ants are not part of the four basic food groups.

But I tried not to think about that as I looked through the little window of the microwave oven. Inside the bag, the ants slowed down a lot and then stopped. Then the chocolate began melting around them.

It was great! I had accidentally stumbled on the perfect recipe for chocolate-covered ants. I figured all I had to do now was wait a little bit longer, so that everything would melt into one big ant-and-chocolate puddle. Then I'd let it cool, and I could have a — well, *feast* wasn't exactly what I'd call it. I gave Adam a big mean smile.

Just then something weird happened. It happened so fast I almost missed it. The only thing that made me think anything was wrong was this little *poof!* sound inside the oven.

I looked through the oven window. That little *poof!* sound had made one big mess. The bag had burst open. The chocolate had exploded. There were chocolate and ants and ant-covered chocolate and chocolate-covered ants all over the ceiling and floor and walls of the microwave oven. It looked truly disgusting.

Adam howled with laughter. "Are you going to be in trouble now!"

I couldn't believe it! Just my luck! Nothing else ever exploded in the microwave oven, except one time when Mom made pudding. I had no idea why it had happened, except maybe the plastic bag was sealed too tight. I just hoped I could get everything cleaned up before Mom got home.

I opened the oven door. What I saw was the worst mess in history. I mean, it would have been bad enough if it had just been gooey chocolate all over the inside of the oven. And it would have been worse if it had been chocolate that had cooled off and turned hard, the way it was doing now. But when the chocolate had ants inside it and the oven had ants all over it — now, that was truly gross!

"You are really going to get it!" my brother sang gleefully.

"We'll see who gets what," I muttered, grabbing some sponges and a bottle of liquid cleaner. "Just shut up and go away."

"I'm not going anywhere. I want to watch you be stupid. This is almost as stupid as saying people eat chocolate-covered ants."

Now I was really angry. At Adam, for sure, but at myself, too. "Oh, yeah?" I said. "Well, watch this!"

I scraped some of the hardened chocolate off the wall of the microwave oven. I held it out toward Adam. "Yuck!" he cried. "It's full of dead ants!"

"Right. Now watch!"

I was so angry I didn't even think about what I was doing as I shoved the ant-filled chocolate into my mouth. Then I bit down on it. The first taste wasn't too bad. It was kind of crunchy — like chocolate with nuts in it.

"Pee-yew!" Adam screamed. "I can't believe you're eating it!"

I just smiled and nodded. The second taste wasn't too bad, either. I chewed some more. I could sense another taste in there with the chocolate. It was kind of a soapy, bitter, putrid taste — maybe some of the acid some ants spray on their enemies. And that bad taste grew stronger with each crunch. Now I knew why chocolate-covered ants weren't exactly the most popular treat on the planet.

"Yuck, Max! That is really disgusting!"

I was beginning to think so, too. The ants were tasting soapier, bitterer, more putrid. But I could handle that. So far.

"You're not going to swallow them!" Adam exclaimed. "That would be *so* stupid!"

I was already not feeling too hot, but a bet was a bet. I was pretty sure I could swallow the ants. I just didn't know exactly how. I decided to concentrate on the chocolate and pretend the ants weren't even there. I got ready. I gulped. I swallowed.

"You're going to be sick," Adam said. "You're going to throw up."

It all went down. I opened my mouth to show Adam what wasn't there anymore. I stuck out my tongue at him. "All gone," I said.

There was a weird aftertaste in my mouth. I ran to the sink and drank a big glass of water. And another. And another. I figured if there was any horrible poison in the ants, the water might dilute it. I drank two more glasses just to make sure.

When I finished one last glass I turned to Adam and smiled. "You owe me thirteen dollars."

"No, I don't," Adam said firmly.

"What do you mean, no, you don't?" I shouted. "You just saw me eat those ants."

"The bet was that you were going to prove *people* eat chocolate-covered ants."

"Very funny," I said. "What am I, an orangutan?"

"Yeah."

"Adam," I said, "I ate the ants, and you owe me thirteen dollars."

"You're not people."

"Cut it out, Adam."

"You're not. You're a person."

"Huh?" I said suspiciously.

"You didn't say you'd show me *one* person ate chocolate-covered ants. I knew *you'd* be stupid enough to eat them."

"Adam . . . " I growled.

"You said you'd show me *people* ate them. Well, you're just one person. So now you've got to show me somebody else who'll do it."

He was right, of course. If you really wanted to get technical, that was the bet, all right. But getting tricked by your little brother isn't easy to take. "Adam . . . " I rumbled. But before I got the chance to finish, I could hear the front door opening.

"Mom's home." Adam flashed me his nastiest, most devilish grin. "Why don't you tell her about the bet?"

Seven

I closed the microwave oven door to stall for time. Maybe Mom wouldn't see the mess.

"So how was your day?" she asked as she put her purse on the kitchen table.

I just shrugged. So did Adam.

"Well, mine was terrible. I'm beat. What's this?" She pointed to the sponge and liquid cleaner on the counter. "You planning a surprise cleanup? Or — hmmm — did you make some kind of mess and clean it up already?"

"Max made something special," said Adam. If looks could kill, the one I gave Adam would've nailed him cold.

"Really?" Mom turned toward me. "What?"

"It's in the microwave," Adam told her with a

grin that I wanted to smash. Sometimes that kid is just too much.

"Let's see," Mom said. She whirled around and opened the door to the microwave oven.

You know how people write "Her jaw dropped"? Well, that is what happened with Mom. Her jaw just dropped. And stayed there. She stood there with her mouth open for the longest ten seconds in the history of my life. Then she screamed. "Ants! And a ripped-up plastic bag! And brown stuff all over the place!"

"Max *says* it's chocolate," Adam said calmly.

"Well, thank heaven for that! Chocolate. Chocolate-covered ants! Adam, how could you do this to Thom and Harry and Willoughby and the rest?"

"I didn't do it!" Adam protested. "I'm not the ant-killer around here. Ask Max."

Mom turned to me with fire in her eyes. She folded her arms across her chest and shook her head. "Okay, Max. What's your story?"

I didn't know exactly what to say. How do you tell your mom you were trying to make chocolate-covered ants and they blew up? Especially without revealing the bet and losing it? "It was an experiment," I said.

"What kind of experiment?" Mom demanded. "You were trying to roast Adam's ants? Bake them? What?"

"Those aren't Adam's ants. They're ants from the front yard."

Mom slapped herself on the forehead. "Oh, great! Next thing you'll tell me you were trying to turn our microwave oven into another ant colony."

I looked over at the oven. "I was just trying to clean them up. That's why there's all that cleaning stuff on the table."

"Clean them up? How do I know the ants didn't escape? How do I know the kitchen isn't swarming with ants right now? Maybe they're already living in the microwave."

"Yuck!" Adam said.

"Couldn't be," I insisted. "I'm positive. The ants and the chocolate were all inside the plastic bag when it exploded. They were good and dead by the time it happened."

Mom let out a big sigh. "Chocolate-covered ants. Chocolate-covered ants. You know, I'm very tempted to make you *eat* those ants."

"Don't worry," said Adam. "He already did."

Mom's jaw dropped even further. She turned to me. "You didn't, Max! Tell me you didn't."

I looked away.

"Max, what am I doing wrong? I know you get enough food around here, and you certainly get more than your share of chocolate. But I haven't served ants. Is this something I should do? Are ants an important part of your diet? Are they one of the basic food groups? Should we have ants once a week, maybe on Sundays?" Sometimes Mom has a very weird sense of humor.

She put her hand on my forehead. "Do you feel all right?"

I nodded.

"No symptoms? The ants didn't make you sick?"

I shook my head.

"All right, Max," she said. "If I hear the rest of this, *I* may get sick. What could possibly have been in your head I will never know. If you feel sick later on, I want you to tell me about it. Right?"

I nodded.

"In the meantime I want that microwave oven spotless. Now! Get going."

Mom patted me on the butt and left the room. Adam started giggling. His giggles turned into belly laughs as he walked away, howling at me. Dumb brothers!

I picked up the sponge and squirted some cleaner on it. Then I got a better idea.

I took out a knife and a plate. I used the knife to scrape the chocolate-covered ants off the walls of the microwave oven — making sure not to scrape up any of the plastic bag with them. I put most of the ants on the plate, and when I was done, I covered them with plastic wrap so they'd stay fresh.

Then I really went to work scraping down the microwave oven. The chocolateless ants and ant-less chocolate went down the disposer. The melted plastic went into the trash can. Finally I used the sponge to wipe down the inside of the oven. I actually managed to get it spotless — well, almost.

When I finished all that, I took the plate of ants up to my room. If I still needed to get somebody else to eat chocolate-covered ants, it was going to be handy to have some around.

I put the plateful of ants on my desk. I must have stared at it for about five minutes. I kept thinking that Adam was pretty smart for a little brother. I couldn't believe how he had gotten the better of me in this deal. I decided to hide the plate under the bed.

At least I had the ants. Now all I needed was somebody who'd eat them in front of Adam. I decided to get some advice from Larry. He had more experience with chocolate-covered ants than anybody else I knew.

"What's shakin'?" Larry asked. Larry and I always ask each other "What's shakin'?" We think it's cool.

"The Empire State Building in an earthquake," I said. "You want to help me out?"

"I told you, those ants my parents had are long gone. You're out of luck."

"I'm not talking about those ants. I'm talking about totally different ants. Fresh ones. Not that stale canned stuff your parents had."

"Huh?"

"I just made up my own batch."

"When?"

"Just now."

"You made your own chocolate-covered ants? You're kidding!"

"Come on over and see for yourself."

"Yuck! Gross!"

"Not as bad as all that. I even ate some."

"Did you do it in front of Adam?"

"Sure. That was the whole point."

"So you won your bet. Did he pay up?"

I hesitated before I said, "Uh, not yet."

"I knew he'd welsh out. I told you. How'd they taste?"

"Delicious," I fibbed. "Kind of like chocolate-covered almonds, only a little different."

"Only putrid, you mean."

"Really, they weren't bad at all. I've got some left. You can come over and try some."

"You *are* kidding."

"I thought you told me you wanted to try those ones your parents used to have."

"Sure. They came in a can. They used some kind of special ants — not ants that came from somebody's garden after strolling around in the garbage can and diving around in the gutter. I don't like the idea of eating homemade chocolate-covered ants. I don't like it one bit."

"These are fresher," I pointed out.

"I'm not so sure that's a plus when it comes to eating ants," Larry replied.

"And they're microwaved. Like popcorn."

"Ants are a long way from popcorn."

"You won't even try them?"

"Not me. Nobody ever said *I* was crazy."

I sighed. This called for drastic measures. "Look, I'm going to tell you a secret. You promise not to tell?"

"Sure. Why?"

"This is really embarrassing."

"Great! So what is it? Something dirty?"

"Swear first. Not anybody. Not a soul. You swear?"

"Sure."

"Say it."

"Say what?"

"Say you swear not to tell the secret I'm going to tell you."

"You swear not to tell the secret I'm going to tell you."

"Very funny. Seriously, Larry."

"Look, I already told you I swear it. Now tell me the secret."

"Oh, all right." I told him the reason my brother hadn't paid me yet and why I had to get somebody else to eat the ants.

"Man! That little brother of yours is really sharp! He outsmarted you!"

"Don't rub it in or anything."

"Wait till I tell the guys!"

"This is a secret. You promised not to tell."

"Yeah," Larry remembered. "Well, I'll think about it."

"So look," I said. "How about if we split the

money. Six-fifty for me and six-fifty for you?"

"To not tell the guys?"

"You already swore you wouldn't tell the guys."

"Sort of."

"You did. Now I'm offering you money to eat a few measly chocolate-covered ants. Think about it."

"For six dollars? And risk getting ant poisoning or something?"

"Six-fifty," I reminded him.

"Forget it! I wouldn't eat ants for a million dollars."

"Okay. A million and one dollars," I said. "My final offer."

"Very funny," Larry sniffed. "But even if you had the money, I'd still say no."

"Some friend you are!" I hung up the phone.

I made a few more calls before dinner. It was amazing. Somehow my other friends had already heard about how my little brother had tricked me. They thought it was a riot. I didn't have to guess how they'd found out. I knew I'd have to get even with Larry somehow.

But what was worse was that nobody wanted to eat the ants. I even went up as high as nine dollars. If I won the bet, I could take the nine out of my winnings and still come out four dollars ahead, which was still better than handing over the thirteen, which I didn't have anyway. But nobody was willing to eat my ants. Nobody even wanted to look at them.

I took the plate out from under the bed and stared at it. There had to be a way to do this. There just had to. Somebody on the planet ought to be willing to eat a few measly chocolate-covered ants for nine dollars. But I couldn't think of who.

Then I remembered Dennis Ball. Dennis was a little kid, a friend of my brother's. I remembered him from one of my brother's birthday parties. The reason I remembered him was that this kid actually ate banana skins. Also peanut shells. He was sort of famous for it. He said he liked them.

I figured if there was one kid who would eat chocolate-covered ants, it was Dennis Ball. I didn't have his phone number. But he had that weird name — I mean, I don't even have to tell you what people called him, right? — so he was easy to remember. There were only maybe fifteen "Balls" in the phone book and only one in our neighborhood. So I was pretty sure I had the right number when I phoned.

"Is Dennis there?"

"Who's calling?"

"Max Musselman." (Yeah, I know. I've got a weird name, too. Don't get started on it, okay?)

"Dennis! It's for you! Somebody named Max!"

Dennis picked up the phone. "Yeah?"

"This is Max Musselman," I said. "Adam's brother?"

"Oh, yeah. What do you want?"

"Do you still eat banana peels? And peanut shells?"

"Sure. They're great."

I couldn't believe my luck. "How'd you like to make five dollars?"

"What do I have to do for it?"

"Eat something."

"That's all?"

"Yeah."

"I love to try new stuff. Is it something people don't usually eat?"

"Well, uh, sort of."

"Great! When do you want me to do this?"

"Probably tomorrow, when my brother's around."

"Sure."

"Say, after school? Could you come over here?"

"I'll need a ride home."

"Sure. My mom'll take you."

"Great! This'll be fun. You're trying to gross your brother out or something?"

"Sort of."

"You don't want me to eat his ants — those ones he's always talking about — do you?"

"No, not exactly."

"Well, whatever it is, it sounds good to me."

"Me, too, Dennis. See you tomorrow."

"Oh, yeah, one thing."

"What?"

"There's not any chocolate in it, is there? I'm real allergic to chocolate. If I eat even a little teensy bit, I start gasping for air, and then I break out in these big hives, and then I have to take these shots and — "

I hung up the phone. No wonder he ate all that other junk! Allergic to chocolate! Poor kid! And worse: poor me!

Eight

THAT night we had leftover lasagna for dinner. "Yuck!" Adam grunted. "I'm not touching this stuff!"

Mom sighed. "Adam, this is the same 'stuff' you loved last week."

"Last week you didn't heat it up in a microwave oven that had lots of filthy ants in it," Adam said.

Mom scowled. "Come on, Adam, eat. Max cleaned the oven."

Adam kept lifting the lasagna noodles and looking for trouble. "Maybe some ants got caught in the cracks."

"The only cracks are in your head," I said. "There aren't any ants in the oven. Or in this lasagna, either."

Adam made a face. "Yuck. I see one."

Mom leaned over the table. "Where?"

Adam pointed to a dark little fleck on top of the lasagna. "That's oregano, Adam," Mom told him. "Oregano. A spice. It was in there last week, too."

"Last week I didn't have to worry that it might be an ant." Adam dangled his fork over the dark fleck. "You sure this isn't an ant?"

"Positive," Mom said. She stuck her fork into Adam's lasagna, stabbed a hunk that included the oregano fleck, and ate it. "Satisfied?"

Adam rolled his eyeballs. "I guess."

"Adam, if you don't eat that lasagna, I will," I said.

"Sure you will. You'd eat it even if it did have ants in it."

"Look, Adam, I'm getting tired of this," Mom said. "Either eat your food or don't. But shut up about it, okay?"

Adam cut off a tiny piece of lasagna and stuck it in his mouth. "Antsagna," I mumbled.

Adam spat it out. "And that's enough out of you, Max," Mom said.

It was kind of fun teasing my brother. But if I didn't find somebody else to eat ants, he was going to have the last laugh.

And I knew it wasn't going to be easy. I didn't need somebody to eat a *lot* of ants — just a few, ones that were tastefully coated in fine milk chocolate. But I knew it was going to be hard to find somebody all the same.

I thought about it until I fell asleep. I even dreamed about it — or was that just some ants acting up in my stomach?

Next morning, I decided the best idea was to take some of my ants to school. It would never work just to ask somebody to eat chocolate-covered ants. But maybe if they saw how easy it was for me — if I could *pretend* it was easy — then they'd do it themselves on a dare or something.

So I took a plastic bag from the kitchen up to my bedroom. I took the plate from under my bed. The chocolate-covered ants looked okay — or at least as okay as they could look. I put about half of them into the bag, sealed it up, and stuck it in my pocket. Then I covered the plate again and shoved it back under the bed.

Larry was the first person I ran into at the lockers. "What's shakin'?" he asked.

"Our secret, that's what," I said in a nasty tone. "You shook it till it broke. Thanks a lot."

"Anytime," he told me. "Anytime. Hey, did you find somebody to eat your ants?"

This guy Brian Innamorato overheard and came over. "Eat what?" he asked.

"Ants," I said.

"You're kidding!" Brian was already bigger than Larry and me put together, and all muscle. He's planning to be a football star. Usually he doesn't have much to do with us, but now he seemed really interested.

"Want to bet?" I pulled the bagful of chocolate-covered ants out of my pocket.

Brian and Larry took a closer look. "Gross!" Brian said. "First-class gross! You want somebody to *eat* these?"

"Yeah," I said. "I dare you."

"Forget it," said Brian. "Daring's for little kids."

"Don't fall for that one," Larry told him. "If you're willing to eat those things, Max will pay you to do it."

I glared at him. Of all the best friends in the world, I had to pick this one!

"How much?" Brian asked.

"Five dollars," I said.

"Hold out for six-fifty," Larry advised. I wanted to brain him.

"Let me see 'em," Brian said.

I handed him the bag. He opened it up and gave the ants a sniff. "Doesn't smell so bad."

"It's not," I told him. "I ate some yesterday."

"Let's see you eat some more," Larry urged.

"Yeah," Brian agreed.

"Okay." I moved toward the water fountain. I knew I'd need it pretty soon.

"We're waiting," Larry said.

"Okay, okay." I broke off a hunk of the chocolate and held it out toward them. "Look. You agree there are ants in there?"

"Yeah, we see 'em," Brian said.

"If they *are* ants," Larry added. "Maybe they're just almonds or something shaped like ants."

"Taste some and find out," I said, holding some of the ants out toward him. "Come on, go ahead."

"Not me," Larry said.

"Yeah, right," I told him. "Mr. Brave."

"We still haven't seen *you* do it," he reminded me.

So I took a deep breath and stuck a hunk of chocolant in my mouth. Somehow it didn't taste as bad as it had tasted the day before. Or maybe that was because I knew what to expect. First the chocolate. Then the soapy, bitter, putrid taste. Then the taste getting worse. Then ignoring it and swallowing hard.

I did it. I've done worse things in my life.

"You ate it!" Larry exclaimed. "You actually ate it! Max Musselman eats chocolate-covered ants!" he shouted up and down the hall. "Max Musselman eats chocolate-covered ants!"

"You want to try?" I asked them.

"For five dollars?" Brian said. "Sure. Why not?"

"You can try them now for free if you want," I said. "But if you want the five dollars, you have to come over to my house after school today." And I explained all about the bet with my little brother. I left out the part about how he'd outsmarted me. I figured Brian would hear all about that from Larry soon enough.

"Okay," Brian said. "We'll meet by your bus after school. If you can eat those things, I can."

"Great!" I said. I felt terrific. I had Adam right

where I wanted him. Brian would eat the ants. I would win my bet. Nothing could stop me now!

But when Larry and Brian were out of sight I ran to the fountain. Wouldn't you know it! Out of order! And the nearest one was miles down the hall, and now the late bell was ringing.

My mouth and stomach didn't feel any too great, but my mind was kind of dancing and singing as I went down the hall to homeroom. Brian was going to solve my problem. There was no doubt about it.

And my ants were getting to be famous, probably because of Larry's big mouth. In homeroom, half a dozen kids came up to me and asked if I really had chocolate-covered ants with me. They wanted to see the ants for themselves. So we hung out at the back of the room and passed the bag around.

"Gross!" said Marcy.

"Yuck!" said Phil.

"I actually saw him eat them," said Larry. "No kidding." Now that I was getting to be sort of famous, it made sense to be my friend again.

I looked toward the front of the room. I just hoped Mrs. Wagman didn't start wondering what was going on. Wagman didn't have much of a sense of humor. But she hardly ever noticed stuff like this. She was usually too far behind on grading papers.

"Maybe those are fake ants," said Phil.

That was exactly what Larry had said ten

minutes ago, but now he was on my side. "They are not. Taste them if you don't believe us."

"Not me," said Phil.

"Gross," Marcy repeated.

But neither one of them ate the ants, and neither did Larry.

Some of the kids in first-period science class had heard about my ants. I just knew Ms. Fisher would give me trouble if she saw them, so I refused to show them to anybody till class was over.

But in second-period math class it was different. Nelson Walker sits a couple of desks away, and he's done me a couple of favors about getting homework to me when I was out sick. So when he passed me a note that read "Send the ants over here," I didn't really want to refuse.

I waited until Mr. Milken wasn't looking. Then I took the bag out of my pocket and handed it to Larry, who sits between Nelson and me. He passed them on carefully.

"Gross! Ultra gross! Grossest thing I ever saw!" Nelson whispered at me. He flipped the bag over and over, shaking his head.

I motioned to Nelson to give them back. "Okay, okay," he muttered, and passed the bag back to Larry.

Then Larry started to hand the bag back to me. The only problem was that Mr. Milken happened to be looking straight at us. "Max

Musselman: Stand up, please. Also you, Knut-son."

The bag fell to the floor between us.

"Musselman? Knutson? Up!" Milken barked.

I stood up. Larry did, too.

"What do you gentlemen have in that bag?" Mr. Milken demanded.

"Chocolate?" I said.

"And were you eating that chocolate?" Mr. Milken asked.

Larry shook his head.

"No, sir," I said. I thought maybe the "sir" would help.

It didn't. "You know the rules about food in class," Mr. Milken said. "Bring that bag up here."

Some of the kids were giggling as I picked up the bag. The ones who knew just what was in the bag were giggling the hardest. I followed Larry up to Mr. Milken's desk and set the bag on it.

Mr. Milken took a look. "And just what kind of chocolate is this supposed to be?"

Larry didn't answer. "It's, uh, just, you know, chocolate," I said. More giggles from the class.

Mr. Milken held the bag up to his eyes. "What are these little *things* in it?"

There was a barrage of giggles behind me. Larry kept his mouth shut. "Uh, ants," I stammered.

Mr. Milken took a closer look. He made a

horrified face and dropped the bag on his desk. "Chocolate-covered ants? Chocolate-covered ants?"

I just sort of nodded.

"Were you planning to eat these?"

"Uh, not really," I stammered.

"What were you planning to do with them?"

Larry still clammed up. I just shrugged.

"Maybe sneak them into people's food when they weren't looking?" Milken asked. "Play a practical joke?"

More giggling. I shrugged again.

"Maybe you'd like to eat some for the class?"

"Not me!" Larry said with genuine terror in his eyes.

"Me, neither," I said. "There's a rule against eating in class."

"Well, I'll grant you a special exception. But let's let democracy rule. How many of you want to see Musselman and Knutson eat a few chocolate-covered ants?"

Every hand in the room shot up.

Mr. Milken turned to us and bowed politely. "Please," he said.

I opened the bag and took out a small hunk. I sighed. I bit into the ants. They tasted just like the first two times, only staler. Finally I swallowed. Everybody in the class whooped and hollered and applauded.

"Your turn," Mr. Milken told Larry. I handed him the bag.

"I don't believe this!" Larry said. "They're not even my ants. They're Max's ants. Tell him, Max!"

"I didn't ask you whose ants they were," Mr. Milken said patiently. "I asked you to eat them."

"But they're not my ants!" Larry howled.

"Eat," Mr. Milken said firmly.

Larry flashed me one of his "I'm gonna get you for this" looks. He rooted around in the bag and found the very tiniest piece.

"Too small," Milken said. "Give me that bag." Larry did. Milken looked inside and took out a nice big hunk just studded with ants. "This is the piece for you," he said, handing it to Larry. The class cracked up.

"Come on!" Larry exclaimed. "This is twice as big as the one Max ate!"

Milken nodded with an evil smile. The class laughed some more.

"This really stinks!" Larry said. He stared at the piece. He bit off a corner of it and made awful faces as he chewed it up.

"The whole thing," Milken reminded him.

Larry put the rest of the piece in his mouth and chewed that up, too. You could tell he was pretty unhappy about it, because he put his hand over his mouth as though he might spit out the whole wad.

"Spit that out and you've flunked the course," Milken said cheerfully.

I almost felt sorry for Larry. He chewed and

chewed, but you could tell he was afraid to swallow. I didn't exactly blame him. But I was also rooting for him; if he ate those ants, I won my bet with Adam.

"Come on, Knutson, down the hatch," Milken said. "We've got some fractions to take care of here."

Larry screwed up his face. There were almost tears in his eyes. But finally he gulped and swallowed the ants. The class applauded. I applauded, too. Thanks to Mr. Milken, I had won my bet. I felt like going up and shaking his hand.

"Thank you," said Mr. Milken. "That was truly revolting. Now please deposit the rest in the circular file."

The circular file was Mr. Milken's name for the wastebasket. Larry dropped the bagful of ants inside.

"Back to your seats, you two," Milken said.

Larry bumped me as I sat down. "This is the worst thing that has ever happened to me in my entire life, Musselman," he said. "I am going to kill you."

Nine

"I want that six dollars and fifty cents," Larry said as we left Mr. Milken's class and headed for the nearest water fountain.

"Forget it!" I told him. "You didn't eat those ants because you agreed to. You ate them because Mr. Milken made you."

"It doesn't matter. I ate them, didn't I?"

"You also told everybody on the planet the secret you promised not to tell. So we're even."

"We are not even, Max. We aren't close to even."

"Well, if you really like the way ants taste, I've got more left at home."

"Very funny," Larry said as he went down the hall to his next class. "We'll discuss this later."

And we weren't the only ones who were dis-
cussing it. Word gets around our school fast, and
that little incident in Mr. Milken's class made us
kind of instant celebrities. All day long, kids kept
stopping me in the hall asking dumb questions
about the ants. It was fun for a while, but finally
I started giving them dumb answers:

Do you really eat chocolate-covered ants?
Only when I can't find chocolate-covered
praying mantises.
Where did you get the ants?
I swapped some Rocky Roach ice cream
for them.
What do ants taste like?
They taste like mosquitoes, only crunchy.
Aren't you afraid they'll make you sick?
Why? Anteaters don't get sick, do they?
Can I see the ants?
Sure. Just go into Mr. Milken's class and
stick your head in his circular file.

Word had even gotten back to Adam. "Now
everybody in school knows how crazy you are,"
he said as we waited after school for the bus
home. "Everybody knows I have the weirdest
brother in the world."

"Maybe I'm weird, but you owe me thirteen
dollars."

"What?"

"Come on, don't play dumb. You must have heard. Larry ate the ants, too."

"I heard about it, all right. But I didn't *see* it."

"Come on, Adam. A bet's a bet. Everybody in my class saw him. Thirty kids were witnesses. You can ask anybody."

"But I'm not gonna ask anybody. I have to see it with my own eyes. That was our deal."

"That stinks, Adam."

"I said you had to prove it. And the only way to prove it is to show me. If he really ate the ants, he can eat them again — in front of me. If not, you owe me thirteen dollars."

That's when Larry came up to us. "What are you two talking about?"

"Ants," Adam said, and climbed aboard the bus.

I took Larry aside. "Adam won't pay up."

"Big deal. I told you he wouldn't. Little kids never do."

"Look, will you come home with me and eat a couple of ants in front of him?"

"No."

"Come on, Larry. Just two more ants! Little ones!"

"How much?"

"How much what?"

"How much are you gonna pay me if I do?"

"Five dollars."

"Five? Yesterday you said six-fifty."

"Okay. Six-fifty."

"Make it nine and you've got a deal."

Suddenly I remembered that Brian Innamorato was supposed to be here to meet me. "Brian will do it for five."

"Fine. Then let that big dumb guy do it."

"Fine. I will."

Larry got on the bus. I looked back toward the school. There was no sign of Brian. And the bus driver was starting to count heads. When he got done, the doors would close. I should have known better than to think some kid I hardly even knew would show up. The bus driver was heading toward the front, and there was still no sign of the only kid in the whole school who was willing to help me win my bet.

"You getting on or not?" the driver asked.

I took one more look back toward the school. Darn that Brian! Darn him! I grabbed the rail and climbed aboard the bus. Darn him again!

I passed my brother and found Larry near the back. "So where's Brian?" he said with a smirk as I sat down next to him.

"All right. You've got me. Nine dollars."

Larry gave me a very ugly look. "That offer expired a few minutes ago. It's now eleven dollars."

There is nothing like a best friend you can count on. "Ten," I said.

"Eleven," he replied. "It goes up to twelve in about seven seconds."

I thought for six seconds about what would happen if I lost my bet with Adam. "It's a deal," I muttered.

"I should charge you more," Larry said. "Just in case I throw up or something. That stuff tastes worse than cat puke."

"And I'm sure you've eaten a lot of cat puke in your time."

"My mother's cooking," Larry said. "Same thing."

When we got home, Adam ignored us and went straight to the kitchen for a snack. Larry and I had a different kind of snack in mind, so we went down the hall to my bedroom.

"Boy, am I glad I saved extra ants." I reached under the bed. "I had no idea Milken would pull something like that."

"*You* had no idea!"

I felt around under my bed. I felt some dust and my old baseball mitt and my new bat. But there was one thing I couldn't feel: the plate with the chocolate-covered ants on it.

I lifted up the bedspread and stuck my head under the bed. I couldn't see the plate with the chocolate-covered ants on it — or even any of the ants. I got up and opened my top desk drawer.

"What's the story?" Larry said, picking up my autographed Texas Rangers baseball.

"I can't find the ants." I took my flashlight and shined it around under the bed. The plate was definitely not there. The ants weren't either.

"They've disappeared!" I said. "Vanished!"

Larry gripped the ball and wound up to pretend-throw. "You sure?"

I shrugged. I didn't want to give up just yet. Maybe Mom had spotted them when she was cleaning up or something. Unlikely, though, when I stopped to think about it. Mom did most of her cleaning in the evenings, and not very often at that, and the ants had been there this morning. Besides, Mom wouldn't be home for a couple of hours, and this wasn't exactly a call-her-at-work emergency. Particularly since if she knew I'd kept those ants, she'd probably make me throw them out myself.

I looked all around the room. No luck.

Larry grabbed my bat. "Your little brother must have taken them."

It didn't take a lot of brains to figure that out. I remembered Adam had been sort of keeping an eye on me that morning.

Larry took a practice swing that just missed my desk lamp.

"Be careful," I said. "Mom doesn't like us to practice around here."

Larry shrugged and took another swing. This time he actually grazed the lamp. "If I break anything, you can take it out of the eleven dollars."

"Very funny," I said. "Let's go find my brother."

Adam was in the kitchen drinking milk and eating peanut butter cookies. "Where are my ants?" I asked him, not very politely.

"What ants?" Adam replied with an innocent look.

"You know what ants," I told him. "My chocolate-covered ants."

Adam calmly took a sip of milk. "Mom said you were supposed to throw them out."

"What Mom said is none of your business."

Adam took a bite of his cookie. It was time to sound a little more threatening. "Come on, Adam," I said. "Where'd you put those ants?"

Larry waved the bat around. "Let's search his room."

Adam looked calm. "If you do that, I'll tell Mom."

"Let's go." Larry grabbed my arm and tried to lead me away. "He's not going to tell anybody anything. He stole your ants. I'll bet they're in his room."

"I'm warning you," said Adam. "That's my room. It's private."

"That proves it," Larry said. "They're in there."

I knew it wasn't right to go hunting around in Adam's room. But it wasn't right for Adam to take my ants, either. I had to find them. I just had to.

"You'd better stay out of there," Adam warned.

Larry snorted. "Why should we listen to a shrimp like you?"

"Because it's my room, that's why!" Adam shrieked.

But by the time he finished his sentence, we were way down the hall. Adam followed us and yelled at us, but we weren't paying much attention. This was war. Larry and I were going to find those ants, no matter what the cost.

Larry pointed to the ant colony. "What about these ants?"

"That's my ant colony!" Adam cried. "Don't you dare touch it!"

Larry touched it just to be mean.

"Aw, leave it alone," I said. "Those aren't the ants we're looking for."

"Maybe we could pour chocolate inside," Larry said. "And then we could — "

"*Noooooooooooooo!*" Adam screamed. He grabbed the colony, pressed it to his chest, and stood in front of his closet. We shoved him away and searched through it. No chocolate-covered ants there.

Adam stood in front of his dresser. We shoved him away and searched through his drawers. No ants there, either.

Adam put the ant colony back on his desk and sat down on the bed to keep an eye on us. We shoved him aside and ripped off all the sheets. No ants there. We searched under the bed. No ants there, either.

Adam started laughing at us. "Ha, ha! I told

you I didn't have them! You probably put them somewhere by mistake!"

"Don't bet on it," Larry said.

"We know you've got them," I told Adam, and began moving papers around on his desk. So far the ants in the colony were the only ones we'd found.

And then it happened. I bent down to open one of the desk drawers, and somehow I accidentally bumped the ant colony with my elbow or my arm or my thick head or something. The colony toppled off the desk. It fell to the floor with a really awful crash.

"Uh-oh," Larry said.

I held my breath. I felt awful.

Adam gave a terrible shriek and ran to look. The colony looked pretty bad from where I was standing. There was a huge crack running right down the middle of one of the clear sides. The dirt tunnels inside looked kind of caved in. It was almost as though an earthquake had happened — which it sort of had. Ants were scurrying around on the sides and the roof of the colony — and just about everywhere else! I just hoped none of them could get out.

Adam bent over and picked up the colony. "You broke it!" he screamed. "You broke it! The ants are going to escape!"

"We'll fix it!" I told him. "Calm down! We'll fix it!"

"You can't fix this!" he cried. "All the ants are going to get out, and it's all your fault!"

"I'm telling you, we'll fix it," I told him. "Just keep your eye on the thing. Don't let any ants get out. I'll go out to the garage and get some tape."

"First things first, Max," Larry said. "Let's find those chocolate ants of yours. I want my eleven bucks."

"Come on, Larry," I told him. "If these ants here get out, I'm in big trouble."

"That's not my fault. Come on. I want to do my stuff."

"Max!" Adam screamed. "They're going to get out!"

"Don't you want to win that bet?" Larry asked me.

"Come on, Larry!" I said. "I've got to take care of this first! And I still don't know where the chocolate ants are anyway!"

"Max!" Adam screamed again.

"All right, all right, Adam." I shouted back. "I'm going to get the tape. Right now."

Larry followed me to the garage. "Are you wimping out on me?"

"I'm not wimping out on anybody," I said, looking for the duct tape Mom put over my bedroom window when the sonic boom broke it. "We've got an emergency here."

"Oh, some emergency," Larry scoffed. "Your

brother's dumb ant colony got dented a little."

"My mom's gonna dent *me* if any of those ants get out," I said, searching through a pile of junk on the worktable.

"At least you ought to let me take a shot at eating your ants."

"Larry, will you wake up? Right now I can't even *find* my ants."

Larry stared at me. "You're going back on our deal? Is that what you're saying?"

"I'm saying right now I've got something else to worry about."

"Well, so do I. I've got better things to do than hang around here and watch you let your little brother boss you around. This is your last chance. My final offer."

"Will you just hold on a couple of minutes?"

"Nope. I'm out of here." And he headed out the door.

"Fine!" I shouted, though it wasn't fine at all. Now I'd never win that bet. My brother would get every cent I had and my entire allowance for weeks.

"Max!" Adam screamed from his bedroom.

"Hang on!" I shouted back.

I found a beat-up old roll of tape. I took it back to Adam's bedroom. "You jerk! You stinker! You crumb!" he kept shouting. "You broke my ant colony! They're going to get loose!"

I tried to ignore him and concentrate on the

job. The crack looked ugly, but it wasn't as bad as it looked. It was one long jaggedy line, but at least there were no gaping holes. All I had to do was stick a big piece of tape on the plastic and make sure it covered up the crack.

"Where are your scissors?" I asked Adam.

"What do you want them for?" he asked suspiciously.

"To cut the tape, okay?"

"Why?" Adam demanded. I guess he was afraid I'd go on an ant-stabbing rampage or something.

"To make it nice and even. Come on. Get the scissors."

Adam reached into the top drawer of his desk and handed me one of those baby scissors, the kind with the rounded blades so little kids can't stab themselves by accident. It worked okay.

I stood the ant colony back up on Adam's desk. It was as good as new, almost, if you didn't mind a big ugly piece of gray tape all the way along one side. I was almost proud of my repair job. Then I noticed that my brother had disappeared.

"Hey, Adam!" I called. "I fixed the ant colony!"

No answer.

I looked out in the hallway. "Hey, Adam! It's good as new!"

Still no answer.

Then I thought I heard some noises in my bedroom. I went to take a look. From down the hall it looked as though Adam was running around, smashing something, and tossing it in the air all over my room.

When I got closer I could see for sure what I already suspected. I'd guessed right about what Adam was smashing and throwing all over the place: my chocolate-covered ants.

I grabbed the plate from his hand. There wasn't much left on it. All the chocolate and all the ants were strewn all over my room. And when I say all over, I mean *all* over: on the floor, on the desk, on the bed, on the windowsills. All over. In tiny little pieces.

"You *did* take those ants!" I shouted. "Those were *my* ants!"

"So what? You broke my ant colony! It's all messed up. Little Anthony and Harry and Thom and Willoughby are going to have to dig new houses all over again. If they don't escape first!"

"Your dumb old ant colony would still be fine if you hadn't stolen my chocolate-covered ants. If you had left them alone, we wouldn't have gone looking for them."

Adam pouted.

"Besides," I said, "your ant colony tipped over by accident. You stole my ants on purpose."

"Did you really fix the ant colony?"

"No. I just said that for fun."

Adam shrieked. "Max!!!"

"All right, all right. I told you I fixed it. And I did. The point is, these ants are mine. You went into my bedroom and *stole* them."

Adam gave me a sheepish look. "Are you going to tell Mom about it?"

I thought it over. "Are you going to tell her about how the ant colony broke?"

"Not if you don't tell."

"Look, I'm sorry about your ant colony."

"Well, I'm sorry I stole your ants."

"Yeah? And what about throwing them all over my room? Are you sorry about that, too?"

Adam shrugged. "Not really."

"Adam!"

"Well, I'm not. And I'm still mad about how you broke my ant colony."

"How about helping me clean up this mess?"

"What about my ant colony?"

"Go back in your room and take a look. It's fine now — well, anyway, it's okay. None of your ants are going to escape."

"They'd better not," Adam said, and headed for his room.

I figured I might still need my ants one way or the other. Maybe I could get Brian to come over tomorrow or something. So I carefully picked up the pieces one by one and put them in a plastic bag.

"Max!" Adam screamed from his room.

I didn't bother to answer. I was on my way to get the vacuum cleaner and suck up the tiniest dusty little pieces so Mom wouldn't notice. That kid was being more of a pest than usual. If I lost that bet, he'd be totally impossible to live with.

"Max!" Adam screamed louder.

I suddenly remembered something Mr. Milken said when he made me eat the ants in front of the whole class. It was what he said about a practical joke.

"Max!" Adam shrieked. "You put ugly gray tape all over the ant colony!"

"Tough!" I hollered back.

I suddenly figured out the greatest practical joke of all time. It would be to make Adam win the bet for me. It would be to make Adam eat the ants himself.

Ten

I took a look at my crummy collection of chocolate-covered ants. All that was left in the bag was a bunch of little teensy jaggedy pieces.

I took a closer look. Most of the pieces that were left didn't even have any ants in them. But a few of them did.

I sat at my desk and separated them out. I still had a chance. I could slip the ants into something Adam normally ate. He'd swallow them without even knowing. Then — just to make sure he couldn't weasel out one more time by saying he hadn't eaten them — I'd show him that there were even more ants that he hadn't eaten. It might not be easy. But it would be perfect.

I peeked into Adam's room. He was talking to his ants. "I'm sorry, ants," he said sadly. "I know it's not the way it was before. But it's not my fault. Honest." Only Adam could make you feel kind of sad over shaking up some ants. But in a way, I actually felt kind of sad about it myself. I was thinking maybe I should just give up on the bet. Until Adam slammed the door in my face.

Mom came home beat again. I didn't mention anything about how I'd broken the ant farm. Instead I concentrated on a more important question. "What's for dinner?"

"Chicken."

"What kind of chicken?"

"Don't tell me Adam's turned you into a fussy eater, too!"

"I'm just curious, that's all."

"Simple roast chicken. Will that be satisfactory, sir?"

"Sure," I said. "Great!" But secretly I was thinking there was no way I'd be able to slip my chocolate-covered ants into that without Adam's noticing.

"What else with it?" I asked.

"Baked potatoes. Broccoli. Okay?"

"Fine." Except the ants would kind of stand out in those, too.

"How about dessert?"

"Well, how does chocolate-chocolate-almond chocolate-chip ice cream sound?"

It sounded as though I should turn somersaults. There was no way Adam would notice that the chocolate almonds and chocolate chips in his ice cream were really chocolate-covered ants. I had to be the luckiest person in the entire world. "Only perfect," I said.

Adam had a special ant fact for us at dinner. This time he told us how easy it was for ants to fix their tunnels when they were messed up by dumb animals. By "dumb animals" he meant Larry and me. But he didn't say that straight out, so there was no way Mom could catch on.

I ate my food so fast Mom told me I looked like a wolf going after that chicken. But I hardly even cared about the chicken. The important thing was dessert.

When everybody was finished and Mom asked us whose turn it was to clear the table, I said it was mine even though it was really Adam's. I knew he wouldn't complain. He hates clearing the table, so he takes forever to do it. And I couldn't wait.

I finished getting everything into the dishwasher. Then I felt the little plastic bag of chocolant chips in my pocket. I didn't take them out yet. This was the most dangerous part of the mission. If I slipped up here, I was in big trouble.

I took a deep breath. "Can I scoop out the ice cream?" I hollered.

"Okay," Mom shouted back, "but none for me. And go easy. That has to last two nights. I'm not shopping tomorrow."

"I'll keep the dips small," I hollered back.

I took the ice cream out of the freezer. I took two bowls from the cupboard. I took the scoop out of the drawer.

I dipped two scoops of ice cream into the first bowl. That was for me.

Now came the important part. I dipped one scoop of ice cream into the second dish. I glanced around to make sure nobody was looking. Then I took out the ants.

I opened the bag and reached in. I stuck a few tiny ants into the ice cream in the dish. It was perfect. Even I had a hard time telling the chocolate-covered ants from the chocolate chips and the chocolate almonds.

I added a few more ants at the bottom, in the pool where the ice cream was starting to melt. Then I dipped out another scoop. I stuck a few more ants in that dip. They blended in perfectly, but I flipped the ice cream upside down just to make sure.

Then came the cleverest part: I added about half a scoop more. I wanted to make absolutely sure Adam's portion was slightly bigger than mine. Just so he wouldn't think any funny stuff was going on, I was going to let Adam choose between the bowls.

I brought them out, one in each hand. "Which one you want?"

Adam looked closely. "I don't know."

It was the first time in recorded history he

hadn't instantly picked out the larger portion. "Come on," I said. "Make up your mind before it melts."

"Don't rush me," he said, inspecting both bowls closely.

"Adam, make up your mind before it's ice-cream soup."

"Okay, okay," he said. And he pointed to the Ant Sundae Special.

Gotcha!

"The bigger one," I said sarcastically. "Naturally."

"You offered," Adam whined.

"You did, Max," Mom said. "Give him the one he wants."

"Okay, okay," I said, pretending to be annoyed.

Adam dug right in. "Did you know some ants spray their enemies with acid if they come too close? Did you know the acid is called formic acid?"

"Yes, I believe we did hear something about that, Adam," Mom said, biting into an apple. "Ten or twenty times already."

"I wish I could do that to *my* enemies," said Adam, staring in my direction.

"Adam, you know how I feel about violence," Mom told him. "You're not an ant. You're a human being."

"Almost," I muttered. Adam gave me a dirty look.

"How's the ice cream?" Mom asked, trying to change the subject.

"Great!" I noticed that Adam was nearly down to his second scoop.

"Yeah, really chocolaty," said Adam. "These nuts are good, too."

"It would be even better if you swallowed before you started talking." Mom got up and headed for the kitchen. "Now remember to clear your plates when you're through."

"That's Max's job." Adam kept on eating. It was fantastic! He was almost down to the bottom of the bowl. He had to have eaten most of the ants by now. I had to stop him before he ate them all. Otherwise I couldn't prove what he'd done.

"Hey, Adam. Look in your bowl!" I said.

"What?" he asked with his mouth full.

"See those nuts? And the chocolate chips?"

"Yeah. Of course."

"Well, look closer."

"Why should I?"

"Because they're *ants*! Chocolate-covered ones!"

Adam dropped his spoon. "No!" he shouted, poking his nose into his bowl.

"I win! Ha! I win!" Sweet revenge! I laughed at him about ten times harder than he had laughed at me when Mom had caught me at the microwave oven.

But it was no joke, and Adam knew it. He saw

the ants in his bowl. He spat out what was left in his mouth. *"Blaaeeeccccchhhhhhh!* Spit! Blah! *Maaaaaaxxxxxx!"*

"You ate 'em, Adam! You did! I win!"

"I did not. I spat 'em out!" And he kept making spitting sounds: "Blech! Blah! Ptooey!"

"You only spat out some of them. But you already ate a whole bunch. You probably thought they were almonds."

"Did not! Blah! Uk! Ptoo!"

"Did too!"

Mom came in from the kitchen. "What's going on out here?"

"Max put ants in my ice cream!" Adam wailed.

Mom leaned over and looked into the bowl. "Where?"

Adam pointed, and Mom looked closer. "Those are almonds, Adam. Almonds."

Adam picked an ant out of the bowl and handed it to Mom. "Look again. Ptoo! Yuck! Blaaah."

Mom held the chocolate up to her nose. "Oh, my," she said.

I giggled uncontrollably.

Mom gave me one of her looks. "Max, how could you do this to your little brother?"

"Adam just ate a few chocolate-covered ants," I told her. "No big deal."

"I *didn't* eat any ants!" Adam insisted. "Blaaah. Chuch. Yech."

"You know you did. Admit it."

94

"That was a dirty trick, Max! (Blah! Ptoo!) You're a creep! (Yuck! Ugh!) But I didn't swallow any of those ants. (Pyoo! Yuk!) I know I didn't. (Bleh.) I'm not giving you any money at all!"

"Then why have you been spitting for the last ten minutes?"

"Money?" Mom inquired.

"We had a bet," Adam said.

"A bet about what?" Mom asked.

"I said people don't really eat chocolate-covered ants," Adam wailed, "and Max said they did. And I was right, because the only person in the whole world who eats chocolate-covered ants is Max. So now he tried to trick me. It's not fair."

Adam started to cry. I knew that could mean only one thing: Trouble.

"Is this true, Max?" Mom asked.

I didn't say anything. Adam turned up the volume on his crying machine.

"Answer me, Max."

"He didn't exactly tell you the whole story," I said.

"You made a bet with your little brother?"

"Yes," I mumbled. Adam was still sniffling and making spitting noises.

"How much did you bet?"

"Thirteen dollars."

"Thirteen dollars! Max, that's all the money your brother has saved up!"

"That's *more* than I have saved up," I pointed out.

"Wait a minute. How were you going to pay Adam if you lost?"

"I figured I'd think of something," I said.

"That's terrible. And it's bad enough you bet with him in the first place. You can't make bets with Adam. It's not fair."

"What's not fair? He plays gin with Gramps. For money."

"That's different. It's not thirteen dollars a game. It's ten cents. And Gramps lets him win."

"Well, I wasn't going to let him win."

"That's the point. He's too little to make bets. And I don't want you getting in the habit of gambling, either."

"It's not a habit."

"Well, I certainly hope not. Anyway, this bet is over and done with. Adam does not have to pay you anything."

"But, Mom . . . !" I protested. "I won it fair and square!"

"Do you call it fair and square to stick chocolate-covered ants into your brother's ice cream?"

I didn't answer.

"Not only isn't it fair or square, it isn't healthy, either. You'd better just hope Adam doesn't have to go to the doctor."

I wanted to explain all the stuff about Adam calling me an ant-killer and stealing my ants, but somehow I couldn't think of how to begin. So all I said was, "But, Mom . . . !"

"No 'But, Moms.' That's it. Period." She turned

to my brother. "And as for you, Adam, you shouldn't get into silly bets with your brother."

Adam sniffled and spat and made a face at me. I made one back. "Enough, you guys," Mom said.

"Aren't you going to do something to punish him?" Adam wheezed. "For making me eat those things? (Bleah! Yecch!) What if I get sick and die?"

"If you get sick and die, I will definitely punish Max," Mom said.

"But, Mom . . . !"

"Otherwise, I probably won't," Mom said.

"But, Mom . . . !"

"Didn't I say something before about 'But, Moms'? And don't you make any more stupid bets. Okay?"

"Okay."

"Now I would like you two to shake hands and make up. Think you can handle it?"

"No," Adam whined.

"Wrong answer," Mom said.

I held out my hand. Adam looked as though he might bite it.

"Come on," Mom said.

Adam grabbed my hand and shook it. "Yuk! Blech! Pee-yew!" he shouted while we were shaking.

"Attaboy," said Mom. "Very gracious."

Eleven

So I didn't win thirteen dollars from my little brother. At least I won the last laugh. All evening long Adam kept going around drinking water and making loud coughing and spitting sounds. Just before bed I caught him apologizing to the ants in his colony for eating their cousins.

But that night I had weird dreams. I dreamed I was asleep naked on the ground. Suddenly a huge swarm of ferocious ants began crawling all over me. A giant ant sat on a high throne looking down at me and the other ants — and laughing. Then in my dream I began to wake up. I discovered the ants walking over me, and I looked super-frightened.

Then I woke up for real. Ants *were* crawling all over me! My dream had come true — except

I was wearing pajamas and there was no giant ant anywhere, except maybe for Adam. But there was dirt all over my bed to make up for it.

I sat up and tried to bat the ants away, but lots of them were inside my pajamas. I stood up. I could see dozens more running around in my sheets.

I didn't know what I could do about the bed, but I knew what I had to do first. I stripped off my pajamas and ran naked down the hall. My plan was to jump into the shower and wash off the ants. But when I ran to the bathroom, the door was locked.

"Open up!" I shouted.

"In a minute," Adam said calmly from inside.

"Adam, I am going to get you for this. I am going to get you good!"

"What's your hurry, Ant Revere?" Adam asked. "Got ants in your pants?"

"Adam!" I screamed. "How could you do this to me?"

There was no answer, unless you count nasty laughter as an answer. I heard Mom coming down the hall. I ran back to my room and pulled on my bathrobe.

"What happened?" she demanded.

I took her into my room and pointed to my bed. The ants were having a dance, parade, and jamboree.

Mom shrieked and ran down to the bathroom. I followed her.

"Adam! How could you do this to your brother?"

"Do what?" Adam asked innocently.

"You know what, Adam. Open the door. And how could you do it to your ants?"

Adam wasn't in a hurry to open the door. "Those aren't my ants."

"What?" Mom demanded. "Adam, open that door this minute!"

Adam opened the door a crack and peered out. "You remember what I told you about that ant colony?" Mom said.

"Those ants aren't from my ant colony."

"Then where are they from? How did they get into Max's bed?"

Adam giggled. "Maybe they went there because they were hungry. Maybe they knew there was a gigantic *crumb* in that bed."

"Very funny," I said. "You know you put those ants there."

"Come on, Adam," Mom said impatiently. "What's the story?"

"I have no idea," Adam said.

"Adam, I'm losing my temper. If you don't explain this in one minute, your ant colony is history. And I don't mean colonial history, either."

Adam sighed. "I dug those ants up in the yard. They're fresh this morning."

Mom just stood there shaking her head. "All right, you two. This is the last I ever want to hear about ants. Adam, you go help Max clean up his room. You two get the sheets and Max's pajamas and the mattress cover and toss them into the washing machine right now. And use hot water. While you're at it, throw in that bathrobe, too, Max. Then get the vacuum cleaner and make sure you pick up every ant you see. Then we're going to empty the vacuum bag together. If there's one more ant in here outside the ant colony by this time tomorrow, you two are going to pay for the exterminator from your allowance."

"But it was Adam's fault," I pointed out. "How come I always get blamed for things Adam did?"

"You put ants in his ice cream, didn't you?" Mom asked.

"But that was all over last night. We shook hands on it."

"That's right. You did. So look, you two, this is the end. You're even. No more ant tricks. Period. I am beginning to get downright angry here."

She really didn't have to tell us that. We could see Mom was totally out of patience. So we did everything she told us. Or I did, anyway; Adam wasn't a whole lot of help with the cleaning. Believe me, you have never seen anybody vacuum the floor more carefully than I did.

"What's shakin'?" Larry asked me after homeroom that morning. "How come you were late?"

I told him the whole story.

"Too bad," he said. "Look what I've got."

He took a little can out of his book pack. It was all dented and kind of bashed in, but I knew what it was before I even looked at it. "It's the chocolate-covered ants!" I exclaimed. "I thought you said your parents sent them to some relative in Greece."

"Right. But the whole thing got fouled up. Something went wrong in the mail or at Greek customs or somewhere. They couldn't deliver the package, so they sent it back. There was a mess of Greek writing all over the box we sent it in."

I stared at the can. "Chocolate-Covered Ants," it said. "Made from the finest milk chocolate and the choicest farm-raised insects. A gourmet treat for adventuresome eaters."

"You want to keep them?" Larry asked.

"Not me. They'll remind me of this awful bet I almost sort of won."

"You sure?" Larry said.

I nodded. He put them back in his book pack.

"Wait a minute," I said. "I've changed my mind."

"Okay," Larry said. "Don't eat them all at once." And he handed me the can.

When I got home, I put it on the kitchen table and went to my bedroom to change. When I got back to the kitchen, Adam was sitting there. He had opened the can. He was eating the ants.

"Hey!" I shouted. "Those are *my* ants!"

"There are plenty left." He popped a couple

into his mouth and held the can out to me. "Here. Have some."

"I can't believe it! You're eating those ants?"

"They're not bad with milk. They're a lot better than those ants you made."

"But you're supposed to like ants so much. Live ones."

"You have an aquarium, but you eat fish," Adam said with his mouth full.

If Aunt Fran asks me what I want for my birthday, I am going to tell her an exterminator kit that works on ants. And also on little brothers.

About the Author

Stephen Manes has written more than twenty-five books for children, including the Hooples and Oscar Noodleman series, *The Great Gerbil Roundup*, *Monstra vs. Irving*, *Some of the Adventures of Rhode Island Red*, and *It's New! It's Improved! It's Terrible!* Kids in five states have voted his *Be a Perfect Person in Just Three Days!* their favorite book of the year.

A contributing editor and columnist for *PC Magazine*, Mr. Manes has written computer books and software, as well as *Encyclopedia Placematica*, the world's first book of place mats. He has also written screenplays for movies and television.

Mr. Manes and his work have been the subject of several public television programs. He lives in Seattle, Washington. *Chocolate-Covered Ants* is his first book for Scholastic Hardcover.

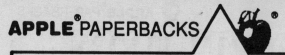

APPLE® PAPERBACKS

Pick an Apple and Polish Off Some Great Reading!

BEST-SELLING APPLE TITLES

☐ MT43944-8 **Afternoon of the Elves** Janet Taylor Lisle — $2.75

☐ MT43109-9 **Boys Are Yucko** Anna Grossnickle Hines — $2.95

☐ MT43473-X **The Broccoli Tapes** Jan Slepian — $2.95

☐ MT42709-1 **Christina's Ghost** Betty Ren Wright — $2.75

☐ MT43461-6 **The Dollhouse Murders** Betty Ren Wright — $2.75

☐ MT43444-6 **Ghosts Beneath Our Feet** Betty Ren Wright — $2.75

☐ MT44351-8 **Help! I'm a Prisoner in the Library** Eth Clifford — $2.95

☐ MT44567-7 **Leah's Song** Eth Clifford — $2.75

☐ MT43618-X **Me and Katie (The Pest)** Ann M. Martin — $2.95

☐ MT41529-8 **My Sister, The Creep** Candice F. Ransom — $2.75

☐ MT40409-1 **Sixth Grade Secrets** Louis Sachar — $2.95

☐ MT42882-9 **Sixth Grade Sleepover** Eve Bunting — $2.95

☐ MT41732-0 **Too Many Murphys** Colleen O'Shaughnessy McKenna — $2.75

Available wherever you buy books, or use this order form.

Scholastic Inc., P.O. Box 7502, 2931 East McCarty Street, Jefferson City, MO 65102

Please send me the books I have checked above. I am enclosing $_____ (please add $2.00 to cover shipping and handling). Send check or money order — no cash or C.O.D.s please.

Name _____

Address _____

City_____ State/Zip _____

Please allow four to six weeks for delivery. Offer good in the U.S.A. only. Sorry, mail orders are not available to residents of Canada. Prices subject to change.

APP59